Animal Rescue

THE BEST JOB THERE IS

written by
SUSAN E. GOODMAN

DISCARD

READY-TO-READ

Simon & Schuster Books for Young Readers

To Matthew, whom I love for his great heart—and his Stylo.

I'd like to thank John Walsh and everyone at WSPA for all the help and photographs that made this book possible. Thanks also to Eunice Greer, Charlotte Mayerson, Deborah Hirschland, and Marjorie Waters for their invaluable comments. And a special thanks to Ruth Katcher and Cylin Busby for shepherding this book through.

Text copyright © 2000 by Susan E. Goodman

Simon & Schuster Books for Young Readers
An imprint of Simon & Schuster Children's Publishing Division
1230 Avenue of the Americas, New York, NY 10020

Library of Congress Cataloging-in-Publication Data
Goodman, Susan E., 1952–
Animal rescue : the best job there is / written by Susan E. Goodman.
p.   cm. — (Ready-to-read)
Summary: Describes the work of John Walsh as he travels the world
helping to save animals in Kuwait during the war with Iraq,
the Kobe earthquake, and floods in Suriname.
ISBN 0-689-81794-0 (hc.)
1. Wildlife rescue—Anecdotes—Juvenile literature.
2. Walsh, John, 1940–   —Juvenile literature.
[1. Wildlife rescue. 2. Walsh, John, 1940–   ]
I. Title. II. Series. QL83.2.G66   2000
639.9—dc21   98-32403
CIP   AC

Cover photo copyright © 1964 Thea Rubenstein. Title page photo copyright © 1965 by Stan Waymans / *Life*. Introduction, page 5: photo copyright © 1995 WSPA. Page 6: map copyright © 1999 Edward Miller. Page 8: copyright © 1996, Comstock. Pages 9, 12, 16, 18, 19: copyright © 1965 by Stan Waymans / *Life*. Pages 10, 11, 13, 14: copyright © 1964 Thea Rubenstein. Page 20: map copyright © 1999 Edward Miller. Pages 21, 23, 24, 25, 28 (top), 29, 30, 32, 33: copyright © 1990 John Walsh, WSPA. Page 22: copyright © 1991 Steve McCurry / Magnum Photos, Inc. Page 26, 28 (bottom), 31, 34: copyright © 1990 WSPA. Page 36: map copyright © 1999 Edward Miller. Chapter Three: all photos copyright © 1995 WSPA.

Contents

Introduction 5

1. *Jungle Rescue* 7

2. *Wartime Rescue* 21

3. *Earthquake Rescue* 37

Introduction

A volcano begins to cough smoke and fire. Police help people escape the danger. But who helps the animals?

During wartime, people suffer. The Red Cross helps by sending food and medicine. But who helps the animals?

John Walsh does. He works at the World Society for the Protection of Animals in Boston, Massachusetts. For the past thirty-five years, he has traveled all over the world to save animals.

John thinks he has the best job there is.

Atlantic Ocean

SURINAME

Pacific
Ocean

S O U T H   A M E R I C A

Suriname

CHAPTER ONE
Jungle Rescue

The island was already tiny. Each day, it got a little smaller. And each day, the water crept closer to the hungry tortoises.

At first, the tortoises had plenty of food. Soon every plant was gone. Green plants covered another island just a few yards away. But land tortoises cannot swim. Instead, they climbed on top of each other to escape the rising water.

By the time John Walsh found them, twenty tortoises were packed on an island smaller than a teacher's desk. Some had already died of hunger. The rest were very weak. They couldn't even pull their heads into their shells.

John and his men filled their canoes with tortoises. Then they opened cans of fruit cocktail. Canned fruit is soft and easy for starving animals to eat.

The tortoises opened their eyes at the smell of food. Some even opened their mouths. But they were so weak, the men had to push the fruit down their throats.

These tortoises lived in the jungle of a South American country named Suriname. Suriname's jungle was filled with tortoises and lizards, anteaters and jaguars. Monkeys chattered in its treetops. Boa constrictors hung over branches like vines.

In 1964 these animals were in trouble. A big company built a dam across one of Suriname's rivers. This dam stopped the river from flowing forward. The water was backing up instead. It formed a new lake that was flooding the jungle.

As the lake grew bigger and deeper, the tops of hills became islands. Many animals were trapped. Some of them would drown. Others would starve to death.

John Walsh wanted to help. Soon he was in Suriname, hiring men to work with him. John had never been in the jungle before. He had to learn fast. The water was rising.

John and his men rode boats around the new lake. Whenever they saw tree-tops sticking out of the water, they took a closer look. Sometimes a sloth clung to the dying tree. Sometimes a porcupine was hugging the last branch above water.

The men brought these animals back to camp. There they stayed until they were healthy again. Then the animals were released in a safe part of the jungle many miles away.

The growing lake covered tree after tree and island after island. It also covered forty-three villages. The people had already moved to a new town.

One day John and his men paddled past a drowning village. Only a few rooftops still stood above water. John saw a small brown animal lying on one of them.

"What's that?" he asked. He thought it was a rat or a squirrel.

"*Pikkie dagoe,*" someone answered. In his language, *pikkie dagoe* means "little dog."

Up close the pup looked like a living skeleton. John could see every one of her ribs.

"Pikkie dagoe," he called. She wagged her tail. She tried to get up and fell. She was too weak to stand.

John lifted her into the boat. He gave her some fruit cocktail. Then she curled up in John's lap and went to sleep.

"Pikkie dagoe," John said softly as he pet her.

The next day, the lake covered the dog's rooftop.

The water was still rising.

The animals weren't the only ones in danger. One night John was alone on the lake. He saw a brocket deer swimming in the darkness.

She will never make it to shore, he thought.

John drove his boat over to the deer. But then what? You need two people to lift a big animal into a canoe. If John tried it alone, the boat would tip over.

John had a great idea. Instead of putting the deer in the boat, he put a rope around her. He began pulling the deer to shore.

The deer didn't think John's idea was so great. She kicked. She banged her head. John leaned over to hold her still.

He bent over so far, he never saw trouble coming. *Bam!* The boat hit a log. John fell into the water.

His boat and its four-legged passenger kept right on going. Soon John couldn't even hear the boat's motor. The only sound left was his pounding heart.

John was ten miles from land. Ten miles! He had never swum even one mile before.

John had no choice. He swam for a while. Then he floated on his back to rest. Swim, rest. Swim, rest.

Suddenly he remembered that piranhas lived in this part of the lake! These fish

have teeth sharper than knives. One bite, your toe is gone, bone and all. But there is never just one bite.

Before, John was scared. Now, he was terrified.

He tried to swim without splashing. Splashing let piranhas know that dinner was nearby.

John scraped his leg on a log. Was it bleeding? He was worried. Blood attracts piranha even faster than splashing.

Then he heard the distant rumble of a motor. Was someone else out on the lake? John listened carefully. The sound never got louder or softer.

It's my *boat!* he thought. *My boat is stuck on something!*

John swam toward the noise. He prayed he could find his boat before the piranhas found him. Finally, he saw his boat caught in a branch above the water.

John climbed into his boat. Now he was safe. The deer was safe, too. John laughed out loud with happiness.

He steered the boat toward camp. This time he held the deer very carefully.

For a year and a half John and his men saved animals. Thanks to them, 2,944 sloths climbed into new trees. Seventy-five iguanas lived to soak up the sun. Four hundred seventy-nine howler monkeys still filled the night with loud cries. Nearly ten thousand animals were rescued. All of them found new homes in the jungle.

All, that is, except one. Pikkie Dagoe went back with John to Boston, Massachusetts. Curled up on John's sofa, she didn't miss the jungle at all.

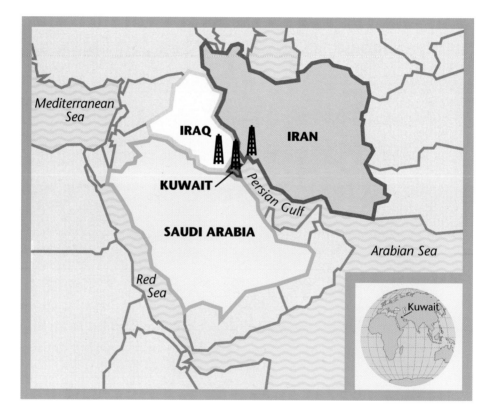

CHAPTER 2
Wartime Rescue

In 1990 a country named Iraq started a war with the country of Kuwait. The sky over Kuwait rained bombs. Iraqi tanks roared through its countryside.

Iraqi soldiers took over Kuwait City. People who lived there ran from the army. Iraqi soldiers moved into the

Kuwait Zoo. The animals could not run away.

The United States joined with Kuwait and other countries to fight Iraq. After seven months, Kuwait City was free.

John Walsh heard that the Kuwait Zoo

was in terrible shape. When the fighting stopped, he went to see for himself.

John had never seen anything so bad. Because they were hungry, Iraqi soldiers had eaten the llamas and kangaroos. But the zoo animals were hungry, too. The soldiers didn't feed most of them.

The elephant had a bullet in her

shoulder. The bear was moaning in his cage. The wolves were so scared, they had dug a cave under the cement in their cage. They only came out at night.

Other animals—the giraffe, buffalo, monkeys, and hippos—were out of their cages. They were lucky. They had stayed alive by eating the zoo's bushes and trees.

Before the war, 442 animals lived in the zoo. When John got there, only twenty-nine were still alive.

This wasn't their war, John thought. *Why did the animals have to suffer?*

John had no time to be angry. There was too much work to do.

The animals had no water. They needed food.

The zoo was also a mess. Iraqi soldiers had cut up cages and used them to block roads. Every pipe and wire was missing.

But the soldiers left something, too. They put booby traps all around the zoo. They taped strings across paths and doorways. If someone tripped over the string, a little bomb would blow up.

I can be careful, John thought. *But what about the animals walking around the zoo?*

Luckily, some American soldiers came by a few days later.

"What are you doing here?" a soldier asked.

"I'm trying to keep the animals alive," John answered.

"Do you mind if we walk around?" the soldier asked.

"Not at all," said John. "But could you do me a favor? Could you get the booby traps out of here?"

The American soldiers got rid of these dangers. Then they wanted to help with the animals. An army truck delivered hay. Another huge truck carried in water.

The soldiers also brought John piles of bread and meat, apples and pears. They even brought brownies and freeze-dried ice cream.

"For months, the animals were starving," John said. "Now they have meat and fresh fruit. They even get cherry cake. It's like Christmas!"

Meanwhile, John was working with the animals. He was trying to restore their trust in people. Food helped.

John drove around the zoo many times each day. The animals began to know the sound of his truck. And the sound of the water buckets. And the sound of John bringing them food.

They also began to listen for John himself. John was always whistling. Whenever they heard him, they got

ready for food or water or a friendly scratch.

Some animals didn't have to wait for John's truck. They weren't in cages. Monkeys swung down from the trees to get fruit. The giraffe visited John throughout the day.

"*E - E - E - H !*
E-E-E-H!" That was the sound made by the African buf-falos. They followed John wherever he

went. They sniffed his back pockets, looking for treats.

At first the hippos were very careful around John. John didn't mind; he felt careful, too. Hippos are very large animals.

How do you make friends with a hippo? John found out as soon as he gave them some hay. The hippos loved it. They ate it. They rolled in it. Soon one hippo ate hay right out of John's hand. And he opened his mouth so John could throw in apples.

John also gave apples to the elephant. He used them to trick her into a trip to the doctor. In this case, *John* was the doctor. He needed to treat the bullet wound in her shoulder.

John put apples along the top of a wall of the elephant's pen. The elephant picked up the first apple with her trunk. She ate it. Then she went to the next one and the next.

John was waiting at the end of the apple line. He had a bottle of medicine in his hand. As the elephant reached for the last apple, John poured the medicine into the infected wound.

One day John heard a crash near the elephant's cage. Someone had left it open by mistake. The elephant was taking a walk around the zoo.

She was also making a mess. She scratched her back on a lamppost. *Boom!* The post fell down. She thought a bush looked tasty. *Rip!* She pulled it up with her trunk, roots and all.

She's a big animal and *a big problem,* John thought. *I can't just shove her back into her cage. What can I do?*

Then John remembered the apple line. He put a pile of apples near the elephant. Then he put a mound of bread down the path. He made many piles of food, each one a little closer to her cage.

John put a mountain of Kit Kat candy bars right in the middle of the elephant pen. The elephant was back in her cage in no time.

One evening John sat at his favorite table in the zoo's picnic area. He was writing a report. Suddenly, a huge head swooped down. A giant nose nudged

John so hard he almost fell. The giraffe wanted to be rubbed underneath his chin.

"All these pets. What else could a grown-up kid want?" John said as he scratched the giraffe.

John looked around. After five months of work, the zoo was clean. The animals had plenty of food and water.

The elephant trumpeted a good night call. Her shoulder had healed. The African buffalo were getting stronger. Two monkeys even had new babies.

John felt proud but sad. It was time to go home.

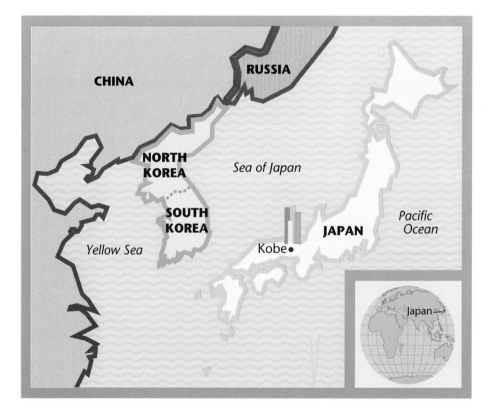

CHAPTER 3
Earthquake Rescue

At dawn, on January 17, 1995, the Japanese city of Kobe was still asleep. Suddenly, the earth began to shake. Buses flipped onto their sides.

The earth shook and rumbled. Buildings fell to the ground. A train station rolled over and crushed the cars in its parking lot.

The earthquake lasted only twenty seconds. It destroyed whole parts of the city. Doctors and soldiers, from all over Japan, came to help the people of Kobe.

John Walsh came to help the animals.

"A dog is trapped on top of a building. She's been up there for a whole week," said a Japanese animal doctor.

"I'll do any- thing I can to help," John said. He grabbed his friend Urs. They went to see what they could do.

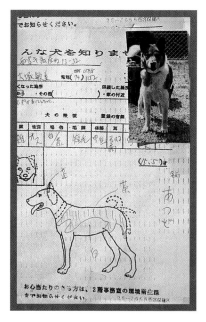

Now I know why no one saved her, John thought.

The first floor of a tall building had caved in. The rest was slowly falling over. Every day the building tipped a little further. Every minute saving the dog grew more dangerous.

A crowd gathered on the street.

"You can't go in," a man told John. "The police are making us all leave. This building is about to collapse!"

John thought about the dog. He looked at Urs.

"Let's try it!" John said.

John and Urs got their rescue supplies. They climbed into the building through a second-story window. Inside, the ceilings had fallen down. Wires hung down like thick black snakes.

John and Urs found the stairway—or what used to be the stairway. Now, it was a mountain of rubble. It was covered with so much plaster and wood, you couldn't see the steps.

R-r-r. E-e-e-r-r-o-o. Strange noises echoed through the building. Metal beams groaned as the building slowly twisted downward.

This building sounds like it's dying, John thought. *We'd better hurry.*

John and Urs began climbing. It was very hard work. When they stepped forward, the rubble slid backward. John grabbed the railing. No help! The railing broke off from the wall.

Fourth floor, fifth floor. Night was falling and there was no electricity in the building. John could barely see. *Whack!* Wires banged into his head.

This is crazy! What am I doing here? John thought.

R-r-r-r. E-e-e-r-r-r-o-o-o. Crash. John heard hunks of plaster fall.

Got to keep going, John decided. *If we don't get this dog, no one will.*

On the seventh floor, John and Urs looked through a window. They could see the dog running back and forth on the roof.

Seeing the dog was easy. Getting her was hard. A deck was still attached to the building just outside the window. There used to be support under the deck. But after the quake, nothing was under the deck but air.

John and Urs had to cross the deck to get to the roof—and the dog. Urs tested the deck with his foot. It creaked. He stepped onto it. The deck moved under his weight. John stepped out too. It wobbled even more.

John and Urs slowly crept toward the other end. They went so far out that, if the deck fell, they could no longer jump back to safety. Then, in one big jump, they got onto the roof.

The dog panicked. She didn't like being trapped on the roof. But she was even more afraid of these strangers.

"The roof is tilting so much," said John. "I'm afraid she'll run away and fall off by mistake. We need to be careful."

John took out a long pole with a loop of wire at one end. He would hold the pole and slip the loop around the dog's neck.

The dog kept running back and forth. John inched forward. Chasing the dog would be very dangerous for all of them. Careful, c-a-r-e-f-u-l, now! John caught the dog! He pulled her to safety. The dog wasn't very grateful. She was still too scared. Instead of licking his face, she tried to bite him.

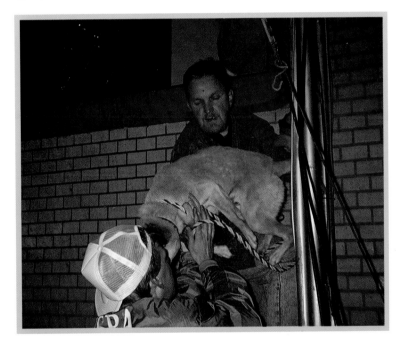

"It's not over yet," John told Urs. "We still have to get back across the deck."

They made a plan. Urs crept across the deck first. John kept the dog in his arms. But he pushed the pole out toward Urs. That way, if John lost his balance and fell, Urs could grab the pole. The dog would still be safe.

Luckily everybody got off the deck safely. Once she was inside the building, the dog settled down.

John pet her. *Now you're happy,* he thought.

He got ready for the long climb down.

Later, John found out that the dog's name was Lager. The dog should have been named Lucky. The building fell down the next day.

John worked with many people to help the pets of Kobe. They pulled animals from crushed buildings. They put out food for lost cats. They set up shelters where animals could stay until their owners were found.

Over one thousand dogs and five hundred cats were rescued. For a while the shelter was even home to four penguins.

When John's work in Kobe was done, he took an airplane home. On the plane, he thought about Lager and all the other animals he had rescued.

John looked out his window at the clouds. Then he thought, *I wonder what my next adventure will be?*